Stella Endicott
and the
Anything-Is-Possible
Poem

Tales from Deckawoo Drive

Volume Five

Stella Endicott
and the
Anything-Is-Possible
Poem

Kate DiCamillo
illustrated by Chris Van Dusen

CANDLEWICK PRESS

Text copyright © 2020 by Kate DiCamillo
Illustrations copyright © 2020 by Chris Van Dusen

First edition 2020

Library of Congress Catalog Card Number pending
ISBN 978-1-5362-0180-2

20 21 22 23 24 25 LSC 10 9 8 7 6 5 4 3 2 1

Printed in Crawfordsville, IN, U.S.A.

This book was typeset in Mrs. Eaves.
The illustrations were done in gouache.

Candlewick Press
99 Dover Street
Somerville, Massachusetts 02144

visit us at www.candlewick.com

Chapter One

On Stella Endicott's first day of second grade, the teacher stood in front of the class and introduced herself. She said, "Good morning, class. I am your teacher. My name is Tamar Liliana. But you may call me Miss Liliana."

Stella raised her hand.

"Yes?" said Miss Liliana.

"Do you have a middle name, Miss Liliana?" said Stella. "My middle name is Suzanne. I am Stella Suzanne Endicott. *Suzanne* is spelled with a *z*. I wish I had more *z*'s in my name, but I only have the one and it's kind of hidden in the middle. Still, I'm glad it's there."

"Thank you very much, Stella Suzanne Endicott," said Miss Liliana. "*My* middle name is Calliope, so I am Tamar Calliope Liliana. But as I said, you may call me Miss Liliana."

She smiled at Stella.

Stella smiled back.

She thought that *Tamar Calliope Liliana* sounded like the name of a good fairy in a deeply satisfying story, the kind of story that Stella's neighbor friend Baby

Lincoln might write — a story with castles and wizards and kings and good and evil, a story with an old and irritated wizard in it, a wizard who maybe looked the tiniest bit like Eugenia Lincoln.

Eugenia Lincoln was Baby's older sister, and she was often irritated.

As far as Stella knew, Eugenia Lincoln was not a wizard. However, she did have a black cat whose name was General Washington. Didn't wizards always have black cats? Or was that witches?

In any case, anything was possible.

That, according to Baby Lincoln, was the whole point of stories.

"Anything can happen, Stella Endicott, anything at all."

That was what Baby Lincoln said.

And so, because anything was possible, Stella decided that she would think of Miss Liliana as Tamar Calliope Liliana, the Good Fairy Who Vanquishes Old and Irritated Wizards.

Tamar Calliope Liliana, the Good Fairy, smiled at the second-graders. She clapped her hands. She said, "Class, I want you to know that I believe in listening closely and speaking softly and singing loudly. I also believe in examining mysteries."

Happily, these were exactly the same things that Stella believed in and because of this, school was a wonderful thing.

There was only one problem.

The problem's name was Horace Broom.

He sat in the desk to the right of Stella.

Horace Broom knew the answer to every question that Miss Liliana asked. And if he didn't know the answer, he acted like he did.

Stella found Horace Broom very, very annoying.

"You don't know the answer to every question," said Stella to Horace on the third day of school.

"Says who?" said Horace Broom.

"Says me," said Stella.

"Stella? Horace?" said Miss Liliana. "No talking, please. Remember, it is our job to listen closely."

Which was just fine with Stella. She didn't want to talk to Horace anyway.

✳ ✳ ✳

In the second week of school, Miss Liliana said, "Class, I have some wonderful news. Today we will begin writing poetry!"

Stella sat up straight in her desk. She raised her hand.

"Yes, Stella?" said Miss Liliana.

"My friend Baby Lincoln is a writer. She writes stories, and she says that anything is possible in stories. I like the idea that anything is possible, don't you? Is anything possible in poetry, too?"

"Absolutely it is," said Miss Liliana. "And a good way to begin an anything-is-possible poem is by thinking metaphorically. Who knows what *metaphorically* means?"

Horace Broom (of course) raised his hand.

And then, without even waiting for Miss Liliana to call on him, he said, "*Metaphorically* means that you can see how one thing is like another, different kind of thing. You compare the two different things, and you do it without using the words *like* or *as*."

"That is an extremely thorough definition, Horace!" said Miss Liliana in her good-fairy voice. She clapped her hands.

She looked delighted.

Horace Broom looked smug.

Miss Liliana said, "Now, for tonight's homework, I'm going to ask you each to write a poem with a metaphor in it. Tell me how one thing is like another, different thing, and you will be well on your way to writing a poem. Tomorrow, we will read our poems out loud."

Stella looked over at Horace Broom. She thought that his smug face looked like a balloon with too much air in it.

And then she thought, *Horace Broom is an overblown balloon, and that's a metaphor!*

Stella had a feeling that she was going to be very, very good at coming up with metaphors.

And also at writing poetry.

She couldn't wait to get started.

Chapter Two

After school, Stella sat at the kitchen table and tried to work on her poem.

Stella's older brother, Frank, stood next to her. He looked over her shoulder. Frank said, "Poems are actually much more difficult to write than one would suppose. Poems are a tricky undertaking. I speak as a journalist, of course, not as a poet."

Frank was on the school newspaper.
He had his own column. It was called
"Franklin Endicott Says . . ."

Frank cleared his throat. He said, "I see
you haven't gotten very far in your poetry-
writing endeavor."

"I haven't," said Stella.

"Well, let me know if you need assistance," said Frank.

"I don't need assistance," said Stella. "I need a metaphor. And I can do it on my own."

Sometimes Frank reminded Stella of Horace Broom. He was the kind of person who always knew the answers. It was annoying.

Stella picked up her notebook and her pencil. She left the house and went down the street to 54 Deckawoo Drive. She rang the doorbell.

Mrs. Watson opened the door. "Stella!" she said. "What a lovely surprise."

"Hello," said Stella. "I'm here to see Mercy."

"Of course," said Mrs. Watson. "She's in the living room."

"Thank you," said Stella. She went into the living room and sat down on the couch next to Mercy.

Mercy was a pig, and she did not think that she knew the answer to every question. Also, Stella doubted that Mercy would think poetry writing was a tricky undertaking.

Stella opened her notebook. She leaned against Mercy. She tried to think metaphorically.

From next door came the sound of Eugenia Lincoln playing the accordion. It was a mournful song. Eugenia played a lot of mournful songs.

Stella closed her eyes. She imagined Eugenia Lincoln wearing a tall, pointed hat with stars and moons all over it. And then she imagined Eugenia Lincoln, the Irritated Wizard, casting a spell that turned Horace Broom into a frog. Or a balloon.

Was that a metaphor?

No, it was just a wish.

Stella opened her eyes and looked out the window. The sky had turned an end-of-day blue, a blue that was almost purple. A leaf dropped from the Watsons' maple tree and twisted and floated through the air. The leaf looked like an awkward ballerina.

"The leaf is a ballerina, and that's a metaphor!" Stella said to Mercy.

Mercy grunted.

"I knew I could do it without Frank's assistance," Stella said. "Frank is always trying to assist me, and I can assist myself."

Stella leaned into Mercy a little more.

It was a very comforting thing to lean up against a warm pig.

Next door, Eugenia continued to play her mournful accordion song.

Stella bent her head. She wrote, "It is good to sit on a couch next to a pig and listen to a wizard play a sad song on the accordion."

Stella looked out the window. Another ballerina leaf danced to the ground. Stella wrote, "Outside, leaves are ballerinas, dancing to the ground." She read what she had written and thought that it was excellent.

It had a metaphor in it, and a wizard. And also a pig.

What more could you ask for in a poem?

Baby Lincoln said that a good story had to have a main character who was full of both curiosity and courage.

"A poem should probably have curiosity and courage, too," said Stella.

And so, she wrote, "I wonder what will happen next."

"Oh, that's a good sentence," said Stella. "It's full of curiosity and courage, isn't it?"

Mercy grunted again.

And then Stella heard her mother calling for her.

"Stelllllaaaa!" shouted her mother. "Suppertime. Come home."

Stella felt a sudden wave of happiness. It was nice to have someone call you home for supper. It would make a wonderful last line of poetry, wouldn't it?

Stella bent her head and wrote. And when she was finished, she read the entire poem out loud to Mercy.

It is good to sit on a couch
next to a pig and listen
to a wizard play a
sad song on the accordion.

Outside, leaves are ballerinas,
dancing to the ground.
I wonder what
will happen next.
Maybe someone will call me
home.

When Stella was done reading, Mercy let out a long sigh.

"Miss Liliana is going to clap her hands together when she hears my poem," said Stella, "and maybe she will even give me a prize. Maybe she will give me the Best Poem Ever Written Prize! And then Horace Broom will be very jealous. Oh, tomorrow is going to be a wonderful day."

Chapter Three

But it was not a wonderful day, and it was not wonderful because Stella made the mistake of letting Horace Broom read her poem.

"Can I read your poem?" asked Horace Broom.

And Stella thought that the poem was so beautiful, so perfect, that she couldn't resist showing it off in advance to Horace.

She handed him her notebook.

"Hmmmm," said Horace Broom when he was done reading. "Pigs don't sit on couches." He was quiet for a minute. He scratched his head with his pencil. "And as far as I know, wizards don't play accordions."

Stella said, "Mercy sits on the couch."

Horace said, "Who is Mercy?"

Stella said, "She's a pig."

Horace Broom shook his head. "No," he said. "Not possible."

Stella felt her face getting warm. "Yes," she said. "It is so possible. Her name is Mercy, and she sits on the couch all the time."

"No," said Horace Broom. He pursed his lips. "Pigs don't sit on couches. They live on farms."

"This pig lives in a house on my street. She lives with Mr. and Mrs. Watson, and she sits on the couch. All. The. Time."

"You're just making things up," said Horace. "And that means you're a liar."

"I'm not a liar!" shouted Stella.

Miss Liliana said, "Stella, remember. We speak softly in this class."

Stella remembered.

But she did not feel like speaking softly, and apparently, Horace Broom did not feel like speaking softly either, because he shouted, "PIGS LIVE ON FARMS!"

Stella shouted back, "NOT THIS PIG!"

And then Miss Liliana said something terrible. She said, "Stella Endicott and Horace Broom, I am very disappointed in both of you. I would like you to go to the office and speak with Mr. Tinwiddie."

Mr. Tinwiddie was the principal. He was a tall man. The rumor was that Mr. Tinwiddie was fond of yelling—loudly.

"You want me to go to the principal's office?" squeaked Horace.

"And me, too?" said Stella.

"Yes," said Miss Liliana. "Both of you." She opened the door.

"But I wrote an excellent poem about the Sea of Tranquility," Horace said to Miss Liliana.

"Not now, Horace," said Miss Liliana.

Stella and Horace walked through the door. Miss Liliana closed the door behind them.

And then Stella Endicott and Horace Broom were alone together in the hallway.

✳ ✳ ✳

"We have been cast into the wilderness," said Horace. His face was very pale. "Mr. Tinwiddie is going to yell at us because that is what he does. And then he will probably make a note in our permanent records, because that is also what he does. And then I won't get into college. And if I don't get into college, I can't be an astronaut. And I want to be an astronaut!"

"You want to be an astronaut?" said Stella. "Really? That's interesting. I don't know what I want to be. Maybe I want to be a storyteller. Or maybe I want to be a mathematician. I think I would be a good mathematician. I'm very good with numbers. But I would also be a good storyteller."

"It doesn't matter. Everything is over," said Horace. He put his head in his hands. "Everything is ruined."

"Maybe it's not that bad," said Stella. "Maybe it will all work out. Baby Lincoln says that in good stories, the characters face their fate with curiosity and courage. Maybe we should have some curiosity and courage. Doesn't that sound like a good idea?"

"No," said Horace. "It doesn't sound like a good idea. I don't know Baby Lincoln. And this isn't a story. This is our lives!"

A joyful sound came from inside Miss Liliana's room. The class was singing "Jump Up and Do a Tiny Dance." They were singing very loudly.

"Listen," said Stella. "They are singing my favorite song. I love to sing that song." She sighed.

"We will never sing again," said Horace.

Stella suddenly remembered that they had been sent to the principal's office. She felt a sharp little ping of fear. She squared her shoulders. "Curiosity!" she said. "Courage!"

She started walking down the hallway toward Mr. Tinwiddie's office.

"This is the worst day of my life," said Horace Broom. He followed along behind her.

Stella had to admit that it was turning into a not-very-good day.

If she had to describe it metaphorically, she would say it was a day that was the opposite of a poem.

Chapter Four

"Who let you chickens out of the coop?" said Mr. Murphy.

Mr. Murphy was the maintenance engineer. He wore a name tag that said MR. CLYDE MURPHY, MAINTENANCE ENGINEER.

"We're not chickens," said Horace.

"We're in trouble," said Stella.

"For what?" said Mr. Murphy.

"We were arguing very, very loudly," said Stella, "and Miss Liliana does not believe in arguing loudly, and so we have been sent to the principal's office."

"Uh-huh," said Mr. Murphy. "And what were you arguing about?"

"Pigs," said Stella.

"Uh-huh," said Mr. Murphy again.

"Pigs live on farms," said Horace.

"Some pigs live on farms," said Stella. "And some pigs live other places — like houses — and some pigs who live in houses sit on couches whenever they feel like it."

"All right," said Mr. Murphy. He held up a hand. "Okay, okay. I've got the gist of things. Tell you what. Let me show you chickens something. This here is

Janitorial Supply Closet Number One. See how it says so right on the door?"

Mr. Murphy pointed at a sign that said JANITORIAL SUPPLY CLOSET NO. 1.

Horace said, "Is there more than one janitorial supply closet?"

Mr. Murphy narrowed his eyes at Horace. "At this particular juncture," he said, "there is one supply closet."

Horace Broom opened his mouth, and then he closed it again.

"So," said Mr. Murphy, "continuing on with my point, I think you two would find it instructive to look inside."

Mr. Murphy unlocked the door and propped it open, and then he reached up and flicked a switch. The dark closet was suddenly illuminated. Stella saw that the small space was filled with shelves, and the shelves were filled with toilet paper and paper towels and paint cans and little boxes of nails and screws, and big bottles of cleaning fluid.

Horace said, "This is a very nice closet. Everything is extremely orderly and well organized."

"That is exactly the point I am making here, chickens!" said Mr. Murphy. "Everything is orderly and neat. Why? Because there are rules about where to put the supplies. You don't just throw things in here willy-nilly, do you? You have a pattern and you follow the pattern, and you put everything where it belongs. That's how it is with life. Do you get what I'm saying?"

"Are you speaking metaphorically, Mr. Murphy?" said Stella.

"I'm speaking janitorially," said Mr. Murphy.

"I don't think *janitorially* is a word," said Horace.

Mr. Murphy turned his head slowly in Horace's direction. He said, "What grade are you in?"

"Second?" said Horace.

"Right. Don't tell me what's a word and what isn't."

"Okay," said Horace in a very small voice.

Mr. Murphy switched off the light. He said, "You chickens need to remember that the rules are the rules. There's a pattern. You follow the pattern."

Stella looked up at Mr. Murphy's face. It was a nice face. It was a kind face. Stella said, "But, Mr. Murphy, don't you think that anything is possible? Don't you think that anything can happen?"

"Like pigs sitting on couches?" said Mr. Murphy.

"That," said Stella. "And lots of other things, things that you hadn't even thought to imagine."

Mr. Murphy nodded slowly. He said, "That's true. There's always surprises.

There's always things that show up when you don't expect them. There's patterns and there's surprises, and that's good. It makes things interesting."

Horace said, "Well, we can't stand here and talk about surprises and patterns anymore because we're in big trouble and we've been sent to the principal's office."

"Right," said Mr. Murphy. "Good luck, chickens. I wish you well."

"Surprises and patterns, patterns and surprises!" said Stella.

It cheered her up to think about surprises and patterns, and about courage and curiosity, and also about how anything was possible, anything at all. She started to skip.

"You are skipping to your doom," said Horace.

At the end of the hallway, a door opened and then slammed shut. A tall boy came walking toward Stella and Horace.

"Uh-oh," said Horace.

"What are you two babies doing out
alone in the big, bad world?" said the boy.

"We're not babies," said Stella. "We're
in second grade, and we're going to the
principal's office."

"Ooooohhh, the principal's office,"
said the boy. He stepped closer to them.
He was so close that Stella could smell his
breath. It did not smell good. "Let me
tell you babies something. You are never

going to survive the principal's office. Mr. Tinwiddie is brutal. He will make you cry."

"Eep," said Horace.

Stella's heart thudded somewhere deep inside of her. She thought, *My heart is a rock that someone just threw into a cold lake.* And then it occurred to her: *That's a metaphor!* And that thought cheered her up a little.

"Just ignore him, Horace," said Stella.

"Good-bye," said the boy as Stella and Horace walked down the hallway. He waved at them. "No one is ever going to see you again."

"I want to go home," said Horace.

He started to cry.

Stella felt a tiny bit like crying, too. What if they *didn't* survive the principal's office? What if no one ever saw them again?

45

Well, there was nothing to do except be curious and courageous.

"Come on, Horace," Stella said. "Let's see what happens next. Let's go and face our fate."

Chapter Five

The principal's office smelled like new carpet and old coffee and bug spray, and the minute Horace and Stella stepped in the door, a woman sitting at a desk shouted, "Name?"

Stella stared at the woman. Her glasses were low on her nose. She had very big hair.

There was a sign on the desk that said I'M MRS. SHIRLEY. Next to the sign, there was a bouquet of flowers. All the flowers were dead, and the water at the bottom of the vase was brown.

Stella thought, *There is a metaphor for today. Today is a bouquet of dead flowers in brown water.*

"Name!" shouted Mrs. Shirley again.

Horace and Stella both jumped.

"Me?" said Horace.

"Who else would I be talking to?" said Mrs. Shirley. "The door? The wall? Myself?"

"I'm Horace Broom," said Horace Broom.

"Why are you crying, Horace Broom?" shouted Mrs. Shirley.

"Because I'm afraid," said Horace.

Next to the bouquet of dead flowers, there was a box of tissues with a little piece of paper propped against it. On the paper were the words ASK BEFORE YOU TAKE A TISSUE. DON'T PRESUME.

That seemed like a metaphor, too. Or maybe it was just really good advice.

"What about you, little girl?" shouted Mrs. Shirley. "Got a name?"

"Stella Suzanne Endicott," said Stella. "The *Suzanne* is spelled with a *z*."

"Good to know," said Mrs. Shirley. She ripped a tissue out of the box and blew her nose. She sounded like a goose. "Name of teacher?" she said.

"Miss Liliana," said Stella.

"Liliana," said Mrs. Shirley. "Yep."

Stella felt a wave of homesickness roll over her—oh, Tamar Calliope Liliana, the Good Fairy!

Mrs. Shirley looked up from her notebook. "Nature of infraction?" she said.

"I don't know what that means," said Stella.

"*Infraction* means breaking the rules," said Horace. "She wants to know what we did wrong."

"Oh," said Stella. "Okay. Well, we broke the rules by arguing loudly."

"Arguing loudly about what?" said Mrs. Shirley.

"Pigs," said Stella.

"And their proper dwellings," said Horace.

"Pig-dwelling arguments," said Mrs. Shirley. "Sheesh. What next?" She shook her head. "All right. You two can take a seat. Mr. Tinwiddie will be with you when he's ready to be with you. And he's not ready to be with you quite yet. He is otherwise engaged."

Stella looked past Mrs. Shirley's desk to the closed door of Mr. Tinwiddie's office. There was a sign on the door. It said:

MR. J. TINWIDDIE
TOUGHEST SHERIFF IN TOWN

It was not the kind of sign that cheered a person up, necessarily.

From inside the office came the rumbly sound of someone with a deep voice talking on and on.

Courage, thought Stella. *Curiosity.*

But she thought the words quietly and without exclamation marks.

Stella was just getting ready to sit down when Horace Broom looked her in the eye and said, "I can't."

"You can't what?" said Stella.

"Stand it," said Horace. "I'm leaving." And he opened the door and walked out.

Stella looked at Mrs. Shirley. Mrs. Shirley looked at Stella.

"Absconder," said Mrs. Shirley. "I knew it. I could tell it just by looking at him. I've been in this business a long time. You can see the absconders a mile away. You can see them coming." She shook her head. She pulled a tissue out of the box.

"What's *absconder* mean?" said Stella.

"It means he's incapable of staying and facing the music," said Mrs. Shirley.

"Oh," said Stella. "I'll be right back."

"Where are you going?"

"I'm going after Horace Broom," said Stella.

"Ha!" said Mrs. Shirley.

And it was funny, wasn't it?

Because who could ever have imagined that Stella would follow Horace Broom anywhere?

Not Stella.

But then, anything was possible, wasn't it?

Surprises were everywhere.

55

Chapter Six

Horace Broom was running down the hallway. His hair was standing up straight on his head. Even from a distance, even from behind, he looked terrified.

Poor Horace Broom.

Stella wondered if he had what it took to be a good astronaut. He sure didn't seem very good at dealing with the unknown.

"Horace!" shouted Stella. She started to run, too. "Hey, Horace! Wait for me!"

But Horace didn't wait. He ran faster. He ran to the end of the hallway. He ran right into the open door of Janitorial Supply Closet Number One.

Stella ran down the hallway, and followed Horace into the closet.

"Close the door!" shouted Horace. "We have to hide from the toughest sheriff in town!"

Stella turned. She kicked the doorstop, and the door to the janitorial supply closet slowly closed.

There was a thud. And then there was a click.

And suddenly, it was very, very dark.

"Oh, no, wait!" said Horace. "I changed my mind. Open the door. I can't stand it. Open it back up. I have claustrophobia!"

"That doesn't seem like a very good thing for an astronaut to have," said Stella. She reached out her hands in the darkness and found the door. She pushed against it, but nothing happened. She felt for a handle. Surely, there had to be a handle.

"There's no handle," said Stella. "I think maybe we're locked in."

"Oooohh, nooo," moaned Horace. "We're entombed."

"I don't know what *entombed* means," said Stella.

"It means buried alive," said Horace. He was breathing in a squeaky kind of way. "Could you maybe turn on the light?" he said in a small voice. "A light would help."

Stella remembered Mr. Murphy reaching up high to flick the light switch.

"I don't know if I can reach it or not," she said.

"Please try," said Horace.

Stella stretched her hands as high as she could and felt along the wall. Nothing. She jumped up in the dark and swatted at the wall. Nothing. She jumped higher and waved her hands more.

Jumping up and down in the darkness and waving your hands around must be a metaphor for something, thought Stella. *But what?*

"We're going to die in here," said Horace.

"We're not going to die," said Stella.

"Oh, what an ignoble end," said Horace. "I wanted to be an astronaut. I wanted to go to the moon and walk on the Sea of Tranquility."

Stella stopped jumping up and down. She moved toward the sound of Horace Broom breathing. She put out her hands and felt the top of his prickly-haired head.

Stella realized that Horace Broom was sitting on the floor. She sat down beside him.

"What does *ignoble* mean?" said Stella.

"It means that there are better ways, more heroic ways, to die than entombed in some janitor's closet."

"We could pretend that this is a story," said Stella. "We could pretend that an old and irritated wizard who plays the accordion has put a spell on us, and the spell has temporarily entombed us, and all we need to do now is to figure out how to undo the spell."

"Except that's not what happened," said Horace Broom. "What happened is that the door to the closet must lock automatically and so we're locked in, and we can't reach the light and no one knows where we are and we will never be found."

Stella sighed.

In the darkness, Horace sighed, too.

"Do you ever get tired of yourself?" said Stella.

"Yes," said Horace.

"Don't you ever imagine things?" said Stella.

"No," said Horace. "Not really. My mother says that I might be a tad too literal."

"What does that mean?" said Stella.

"Well, *literal* is the opposite of *metaphorical*. *Literal* means seeing things exactly as they are. And things right now look very dark."

"Sometimes," said Stella, "when I'm afraid, or when my brother, Frank, is afraid or worried—he worries a lot—we'll hold hands. It always makes us both feel

64

better." She was quiet for a minute. "Do you want to hold hands, Horace Broom?"

"Yes," said Horace.

Stella put her hand out in the darkness. She found Horace's hand. It was small and scrabbly. She thought, *Horace Broom's hand is a hermit crab without its shell, and that's a metaphor.*

She gave the hermit-crab hand a squeeze.

Horace squeezed her hand back. He said, "Your poem was actually very good. I liked it a lot—in spite of its factual inaccuracies."

"Thank you," said Stella. "You said that your poem is about the Sea of Tranquility. Where's the Sea of Tranquility?"

"It's a place on the moon," said Horace. "It's not a sea at all. But sometimes it looks blue. Sometimes, it *looks* like a sea. An astronaut could walk on the Sea of Tranquility. That's what I wanted to do before my life ended, before I met my ignoble end in a broom closet."

Stella gave Horace's hand another squeeze. She said, "Anything can happen, Horace. Anything at all. That's what Baby Lincoln says."

"I still don't know who Baby Lincoln is," said Horace. "But I appreciate your comforting words."

Stella stared into the darkness. It didn't seem quite as dark as it had in the beginning. Was that because she was getting used to it?

Was it because she was holding Horace Broom's hand?

No, it was because something somewhere was glowing. Something was giving off light. Stella bent her head back. She looked up into the darkness above them, and she couldn't believe what she saw.

"Horace," she said. "Look up."

Horace sighed. She heard him move. And then she heard him gasp. It was a gasp of wonder. It was a happy noise.

67

Up high, on the ceiling of Janitorial Supply Closet Number One, someone had painted a whole glow-in-the-dark solar system.

"It's a surprise," said Stella. "It's a surprise in the pattern. Mr. Murphy must have painted it."

"Thank you, Mr. Murphy," said Horace. "Thank you."

Chapter Seven

The glow-in-the-dark planets were so certain and bright that they seemed to be humming.

Horace named each planet. "Mercury," he said. "Venus, Earth, Mars, Jupiter, Saturn, Uranus, Neptune."

And then he said the planet names again, more slowly. Stella said the names of the planets along with him. And it was like saying a poem.

For once, it was not irritating that Horace knew all the answers. In fact, Stella felt grateful to him for remembering all the planet names in order.

She also felt happy.

If you had told her at the beginning of the day that she would be locked in the janitorial supply closet with Horace

Broom and that she would be holding his hand and staring up at the solar system and saying the names of the planets in order—and that she would be entirely, absolutely, undeniably happy while all this was going on—she would not have believed you.

Anything can happen. Anything can be.

"I love the planets," said Horace.

Stella was quiet for a minute, and then she said, "I love metaphors."

73

"I love telescopes," said Horace. "And maps."

"I love maps, too!" said Stella. "I'm really, really good at reading maps. And I'm good at climbing trees. I like to climb trees early in the morning before anyone else is awake. I like to watch the sun rise from the top of a tree."

"I love mornings the best," said Horace.

"I love the end of the day and the beginning of the day," said Stella. "And I love all the time in between, too. I love it when Eugenia Lincoln plays mournful songs on the accordion. I love it when Baby Lincoln tells me stories. I love pretending that Miss Liliana is actually Tamar Calliope Liliana the Good Fairy Who Vanquishes Old and Irritated Wizards. I love sitting next to Mercy Watson on the couch and leaning up against her and coming up with metaphors and writing poems."

"Mercy Watson is the pig?" said Horace.

"Yes," said Stella.

"Does she really sit on the couch?"

"She does," said Stella. "Also, she eats toast and rides in the car."

"Really?" said Horace.

"Really," said Stella.

"I'm sorry that I didn't believe you," said Horace.

"I'm sorry that I argued with you," said Stella. "Can I ask you a question?"

"Yes," said Horace.

"Do you have a middle name?"

"Yes," said Horace. "It's Burton."

"Horace Burton Broom," said Stella.

"That's me," said Horace.

Stella and Horace were quiet together for a long time.

"I wonder what happens next, Horace Burton Broom?" said Stella.

"I don't know, Stella Suzanne Endicott. I can't imagine."

And then, in the silence and the darkness, and underneath all the glowing planets of the solar system, Stella and Horace fell asleep.

They were still holding hands.

✳ ✳ ✳

What happened next was that there was a great flood of light. Stella woke up. She blinked. Mr. Murphy and Mrs. Shirley and Miss Liliana and Frank were all standing in front of the open door.

"Oh, thank goodness," said Miss Liliana.

Stella sat up. She wondered if she was dreaming.

"Absconders," said Mrs. Shirley. She blew her nose.

Stella decided that she wasn't dreaming.

Horace sat up, too. He said, "Are we rescued?"

Mr. Murphy said, "You chickens gave us a real scare. I'm going to have to change the lock on that door."

Frank said, "I wonder if the two of you would be interested in answering a few questions for the school newspaper."

The headline in the school newspaper read:

80

THE
ROSA PARKS ELEMENTARY
REPORTER

**TWO SECOND-GRADERS INADVERTENTLY
LOCKED IN EXTREMELY WELL-ORGANIZED
JANITORIAL SUPPLY CLOSET;
ALL IS WELL THAT ENDS WELL**

Mr. J. Tinwiddie, school principal, was quoted as saying, "This incident has been quite concerning. I would like to remind everyone that while I may be the toughest sheriff in town, I am also very good at talking things through, and my door is always open. Except for when it's closed."

81

The story also had a quote from Horace Broom. He said, "It was very dark in the janitor's closet. It was claustrophobia-inducing. We felt as if we were entombed. However, it was, I suppose, a good preparation for being an astronaut. Which is what I intend to become. And Stella Endicott and I both ended up learning a lot. For instance, I have learned not to be quite so literal. I have also learned that some pigs actually do sit on couches, as improbable as that may seem."

Miss Liliana was quoted as saying, "Horace and Stella are two of my finest students. We are working on poetry in our classroom. We invite everyone to stop by and read some truly excellent poetry."

Mrs. Shirley said, "They were both absconders. I could see it written all over their faces. After you do this job for a while, you can tell who is going to stay and face the music and who isn't."

Mr. Murphy said, "I would like to officially announce that I have changed the lock on Janitorial Supply Closet Number One, and it is no longer possible for any little chickens to get locked inside."

The last quote in the story was from Stella. She said, "I wasn't scared at all.

I just kept remembering Baby Lincoln's words: *Courage! Curiosity!* And also I kept thinking about patterns and surprises and about how anything can happen, anything at all. For instance, Horace Burton Broom and I are friends."

Coda

And they were.

Friends.

Horace Broom came to visit Stella on Deckawoo Drive. He sat on the couch next to Mercy Watson.

He listened to Eugenia Lincoln play mournful songs on the accordion—and also, occasionally, a few happy songs.

And one night, Horace Broom brought his telescope over and set it up on the lawn, and everyone got to see the planet Venus.

"Can you see it?" Horace said to Stella when it was her turn to look through the telescope.

"Yes," said Stella. She was quiet for a minute, and then she said, "It's beautiful and bright. It's a heart humming in the night."

"That's a very good description," said Horace Broom. "It sounds like it might be the beginning of a poem."

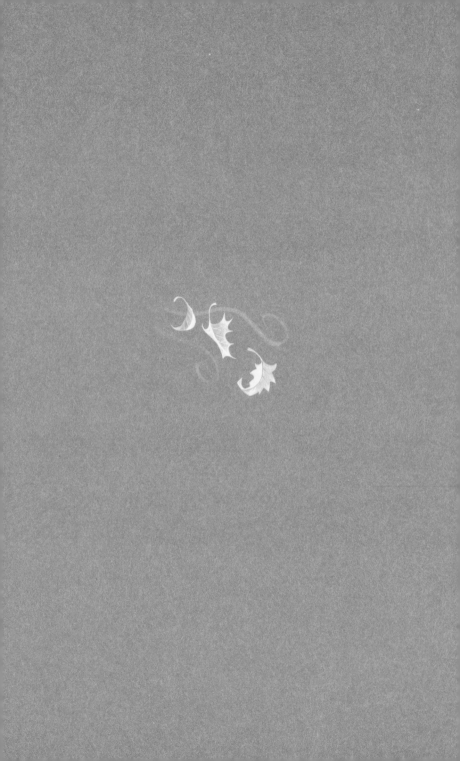